SUPER DEWEY

by Michael Scotto
illustrated by The Ink Circle

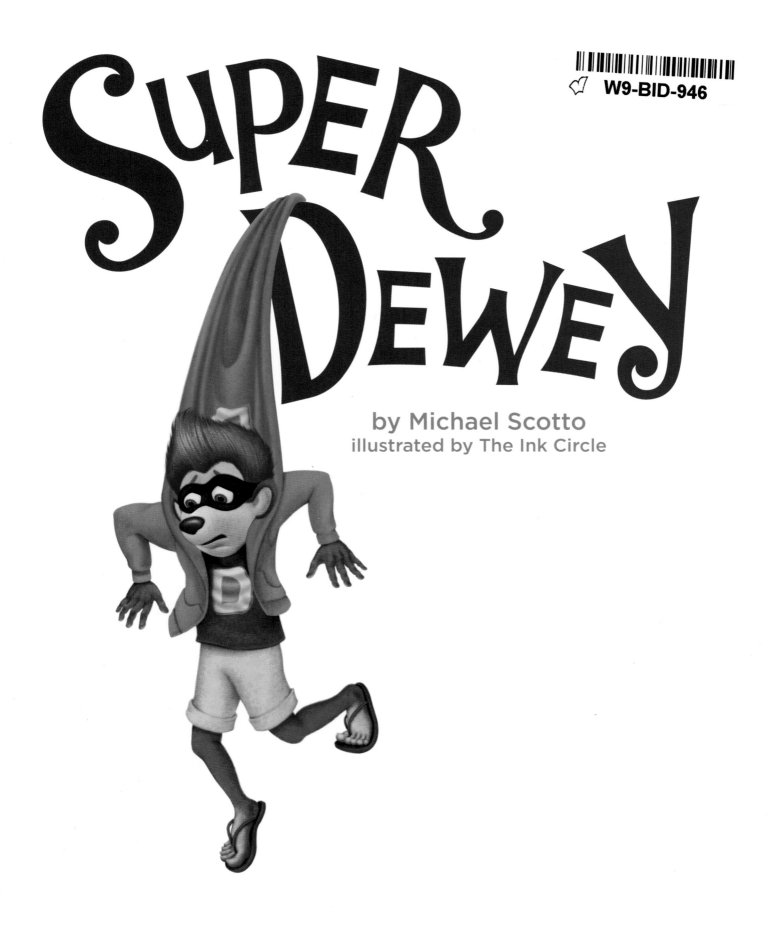

Dewey was the best librarian in Midlandia.

He knew where every book
in the library was supposed to be,
and he'd even read most of them.

**Comic books were
his favorite, though.**

While he read, Dewey loved to use his imagination. **"I want to be a superhero,** like in my comic books," Dewey thought. "That way, I can really make a difference."

The trouble was that Dewey didn't think he was very super. "How can I be a hero? I don't even have a real cape! I'm just a boring librarian."

Little did Dewey know he was about to get his chance.

One night, after everyone had gone home, some mysterious creatures sneaked into the library and spent the evening causing trouble.

In the morning, Dewey found little paw prints everywhere!

"**What a mess!** And oh, no—they mixed up all the books! I'd better get to work."

Around lunchtime, Dewey noticed Star looking through the unorganized stacks of books. "I need your help," Star said. "It's dreadfully important. I have to find this book right away, but it's not on the shelves!"

"Things are a bit of a mess right now," Dewey said. "Come back tomorrow and I'll be sure to have the book waiting for you."

Dewey worked hard all day. "I only have a little left..." he said with a yawn. "I'll take a quick nap, and then...." Dewey dozed off before he could even finish his sentence.

When he opened his eyes, Dewey couldn't believe what he saw. "Oh, no!" he cried. The whole place was wrecked again! "Whoever made this mess must still be here," Dewey thought. "I'm going to get to the bottom of this."

Dewey searched through the books and found an encyclopedia of paw prints. He compared the paw prints the troublemakers had left with photographs from the book.

Soon, Dewey found a match!

"I recognize those prints now! This is the work of those pesky little Inks! **But how can I stop them?"**

"A trap!" he thought.
"I'll hide in the shelves so the
Inks think that I went home."

"When they return, I'll be waiting for them in my **Super Dewey costume!** Then, I'll jump out and scare them away."

"Okay!" Dewey yelled out to be sure that the Inks heard him. "I guess I'd better go home now!" Dewey shut off the lights, stamped his feet as if he were leaving, and slammed the door.

As Dewey settled into his hiding place, the Inks started to creep out of a small hole at the bottom of a wall. "So that's how they're sneaking in!"

The Inks whispered to each other as they scampered toward the middle of the floor.

"Now's my chance!" Dewey thought.

"Halt!" he shouted.

The Inks looked up as Dewey turned on a lamp.

"It is I! Super Dewey!"

Dewey leapt from the shelf,
his cape flapping behind him.

"I've got you!"
he yelled out. "Super Dewey to the rescue!"

But before Dewey could capture
the Inks, his cape got caught on a lamp!
"Help!" he cried, dangling about. The Inks
giggled and stuck out their tongues.

Suddenly, there was
a knock at the door.

Dewey, are you in there?" a voice said from outside. "It's Badge! I was just checking out the neighborhood when I heard a ruckus in here."

The Inks scattered back through the hole in the wall. "I'm over here!" Dewey shouted. "Help me!" Badge helped Dewey down.

"What in the name of Midlandia were you doing?"
"I was just trying to be super," Dewey replied.
"Maybe you should stick to being a librarian," Badge suggested.
"I guess you're right," Dewey said with disappointment.

After Badge left, Dewey examined the library. "What a mess!" he thought. "I wouldn't be a very good librarian if I left it this way. But first...." Dewey covered up the hole where the Inks were getting in, so that they couldn't make any more messes.

By opening time the next morning, Dewey was very tired...but the library was back in perfect order. Soon, Star came looking for her book. "Hey, Dewey, why the long face?" she asked.

"No reason, I guess," Dewey said glumly. "I found your book for you."

Star jumped up and down with excitement. "Oh, thank you so much, Dewey...**you're my hero!**"

Dewey looked at her, puzzled. "Really?"

"Of course!" Star said. "If you hadn't found this book for me, I would never have been able to get my work done."

"You're the best librarian ever!"

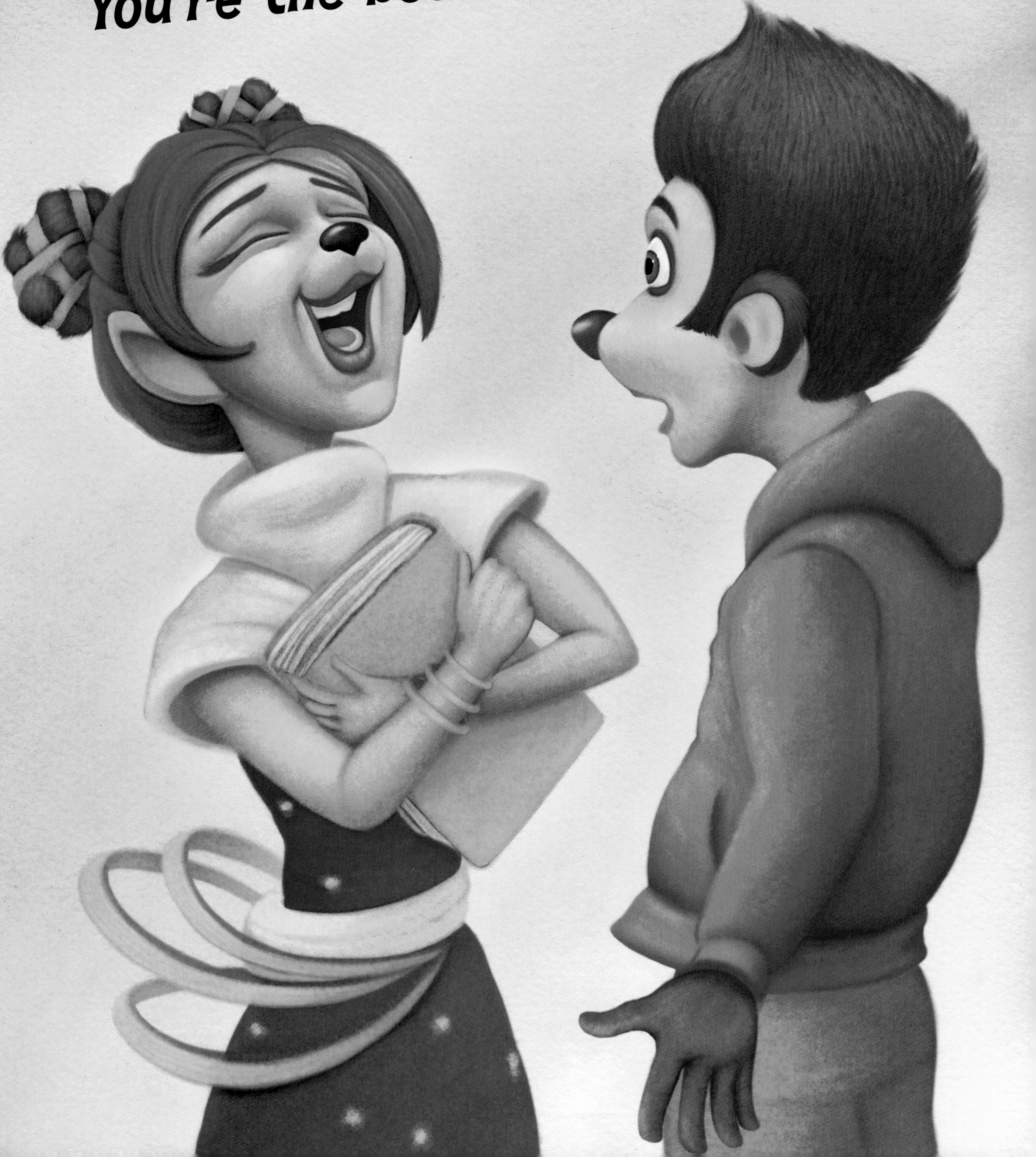

Dewey smiled. "Maybe being a librarian isn't so boring after all," he thought. And from then on, Dewey always remembered that **you don't have to be super to be a hero.**

DISCUSSION QUESTIONS

Dewey's story shows us that everyday people can be heroes.
Name someone in your life who is a hero to you.
Why do you look up to this person?

In the story, Dewey wished he were a superhero
with superpowers. If you could be a superhero for a day,
what superpower would you choose?